TRAIL OF THE CHOSEN

The Story of Cardston's Founding People

By Tom Matkin

With Musical and Lyrical Contributions by Cheryl Davidsen

A Play in Two Acts

Saints of vision led by light
With a spirit that cannot be broken
Hearts of courage on the road of faith
This is the trail of the Chosen
- Cheryl Davidsen

© 2000, Tom Matkin and Cheryl Davidsen
No part of this script or the music in it may be used or performed, recorded, transmitted, published or shown in any way
without the express written permission of the copyright holders.

CHARACTERS, SCRIPT OUTLINE WITH SONGS AND SCRIPT AS AT
July 10, 2000

CHARACTERS:

E. J. Wood - As he was in 1914 - 48 years old - The Stake President

Mr. August Brncich - President of the Kootenay Granite Company

Young Myron Layton - A strong young man in 1914.

Young Matthew Leavitt - A strong young man in 1914.

Charles Ora Card - A short, portly man in his 50s with "duck-legs"

Ben Garr - a "lecherous apostate gambler"

Marshal Exum - U.S. Federal Marshal

Sarah Jane Card - wife of C.O. Card, in her 40s at this time

Fannie Paul - A young lady

Lorin Farr - A young towns person in Logan Utah who offers to help Card escape.

President John Taylor - aged president of the Church of Jesus Christ of Latter-day Saints

Henry Day - Resident of Draper, Utah. Owner of the home where President Taylor was in hiding.

James Hendricks - 40 years old, missionary companion with Pres. Card in the search for a settlement in Canada.

Isaac Zundel - Bishop Zundel age 45, missionary companion with Pres. Card in the search for a settlement in Canada.

Duncan McDonald - Montana Mountain Man aged 30

Sena Anderson (Matkin) - A young lady in her 20s

Samuel Matkin - Age 38

Zina Card - Age 40

John Woolf - Age 40

Jonathan Layne - Age 30

George Farrell - Age 50
Johannes Anderson - Age 55 as a pioneer age 87 in the post office scene
Josiah Hammer - Age 30 as a pioneer, age 57 at the post office scene
Thomas R. Leavitt - Age 45
Hattie Leavitt - Age 28
Ann Eliza Leavitt - Age 35
Sarah Leavitt - Age 12
Sam Anderson, age 9
Slim, A Cochrane Ranch cowhand - Age ?
Billie Cochrane - Son of the owner of the Cochrane Ranch age 30
2 Cochrane ranch hands - Age 20
2 or 3 young pioneer girls - 11 years old
Sister Doolittle - Age 50 and a chatter box

OVERTURE

INTRODUCTION

(Curtain is closed, men are on either side of the stage, heads down and quiet. Sister Doolittle enters through the curtain with great flourish and difficulty)

SISTER DOOLITTLE: Hullo there! Uh, can you see me? I can't see a thing with this light. Hey you up there, can you fix this light. I can't see. I CAN'T SEE. Hullo, is anybody there? Where can you get good help these days? Listen, I'm sure you're out there, I just can't see you. Anyway my name is Doolittle, Amelia MacBeth Doolittle. I'm actually just a character in this play, probably one of the most important, well, certainly one of the most important, but I'm really very special because I'm only a fictional character and pretty much everybody else represents someone who really lived. Oh I have a pedigree and all that. I'm fleshed out, if you know what I mean. I had to have that so I could get into character. You can't act if you don't know what your character is all about, can you? So I know that my father was Adam MacBeth and that he joined the Mormon Church in Scotland in 1846 and that he brought my mother Sarah Smith MacBeth to Utah in 1853. I was only 6 at that time and we settled in Nephi, Utah. I grew up there and when I was marrying age I married Brother Heber Doolittle. I was his third wife. We lived together in Hyde Park, Utah. Sounds pretty racy doesn't it?. Yes, he was a polygamist. He had 5 wives altogether. All at the same time! And 37 children. Actually it wasn't so excitin' at that time cause practically everybody in the neighbourhood had the same circumstances.

We were there in Hyde Park when the United States

Marshals started arresting all the men who had more than one wife. Those were the days. THAT was exciting. Brother Doolittle lived most of 4 years hiding in hay lofts and sleeping in root cellars. We probably shudda got away from there, like the other did, in fact, we was asked by President Card to go north, but we never did. But then this story isn't really so much about those of us that didn't go, it's more about those who did..... (*She begins to exit through the curtain... but then rushes back on stage*)

Oh! I prit near forgot why they sent me out here. I am supposed to tell you that polygamy was discontinued in the Mormon Church over a 100 years ago. Those of us that was involved in polygamy, we couldn't quit it of course. There we were married with children and all! But no more marriages were approved in that way and the next generation left it alone and now it ain't tolerated at all by the Mormons. So iffin you were worried about that funny lookin guy sittin in front of you, you can worry if you want, he is probably the descendant of Mormon polygamists, but it's fer darn certain that he isn't a polygamist hisself. (*Pause*) Are ya? Oh, and you up there, turn these lights around so these folks kin see what's going on, and you people, enjoy the show, and I'll see you a little later when my part comes up! Watch fer it. I think it'll be the best part.

Stage Manager: (*Off stage, loud stage whisper*) Sister Doolittle, that's enough

SISTER DOOLITTLE: You see I have really worked on this part, and I even took a lot of the lines in the script and sort of reworked them, to make them more realistic, if you know what I mean....

Stage Manager: (*Offstage, loud voice*) Sister Doolittle, please leave the stage

SISTER DOOLITTLE: Because, between you and me, the dialogue that was written for me, well, it wasn't really me. I studied the concepts, the emotions, the pathos, the life, the tragedy and the ...

Stage Manager: (*Offstage*) PLEASE

SISTER DOOLITTLE: So you watch for my part, it's in the first act and is it ever good. I was telling my friend (use a name from the audience) just this morning that I thought I might win an award for my part. It's a deep part. Well at least my performance gives it depth and....

Stage Manager: (*Offstage*) Please, Please, Please, Please

SISTER DOOLITTLE: Did you folks hear that? I think someone is calling me. Oh, I think it might be the director. She never seems to know what's going on. I'd better go talk to her, set her straight so to speak. I think everything is okay here now, so I'll just be going now. Good-bye.

ACT I

(Curtain Comes Up, children walk in from back of the theatre and take the centre of the stage joined by girls from the wings)

(Children and Girls)
We welcome you into our circle
We thank you all for coming here
We want to introduce ourselves,
We are the children of the Pioneer

We tell the story of a people
Who were called to blaze a trail
Who accepted and embraced it
With a courage that would never fail

Saints of vision, led by light
With a spirit that cannot be broken
Hearts of courage on the road of faith
This is the trail of the chosen.

(Men)
When the call is made to journey
To a distant promised land
Who'll embrace the challenge
Who will make the stand
Will the hardships of the past
Cloud the path that lies ahead
(All)
Will the trials over take us
With memories of our dead
No!
With the power of God Almighty
No strength will they lack
They'll head out on the journey
- never looking back!

Saints of vision, led by light
With a spirit that cannot be broken

Hearts of courage on the road of faith
This is the trail of the chosen
Hearts of courage on the road of faith
This is the trail of the chosen

(Women & Children)
Saints of vision, led by light
With a spirit that cannot be broken
Heart of courage on the road of faith
This is the trail of the chosen

(End of Song all players off stage: Enter a narrator to deliver this spoken poem:)

Many are called and chosen but few
This is the Word in the Bible
First shall be last and last shall be first
And so with your kind approval

We will begin where our story ends
To show this a journey successful
That the promises that the Lord will give
Reward us for decisions celestial

Listen now as President Wood
Brings a BC quarryman to see
Temple construction in 1914
Shades of what our town would be.....

SCENE 1   (OPENING)

(A group of workmen are shoveling gravel into a wagon. President Edward James Wood the Stake President and supervisor of temple construction is showing August Brncich *around th temple construction scene.   It is 1914 in Cardston, Alberta.)*

Players in the Scene: E.J. Wood, Lethbridge Herald Reporter, Young Myron Layton, Young Matthew Leavitt)

Layton: (*as Wood and Brncich enter the scene*) Welcome President Wood.

E.J. Wood: (*walking on stage with the Quarry President, greets the men*) Brothers, sorry to disturb your lunch time, this is Mr. August Brncich of the Kootenay Granite Company.   His company is going to supply the granite for our new temple.   He wants to see where his rock is going to end up and I'm giving him a tour.   Brother Layton, what number is this wagon?

Brother Layton: It's number 644.

E.J. Wood: Well that's tremendous.   Just wonderful. In two weeks we have hauled 643 loads of gravel to the temple site. At times we have had as many as 32 teams working at one time.   Each hauling a single cubic yard of screened gravel over ½ mile to the site and then coming back down here to load again. How many more to go boys?

Brother Layton: Well let's see.   How much is 14,000 less 644.   I guess we have 13,456 to go. Maybe if we shoveled real fast and didn't stop for any more breaks we could finish it up before dark, what do you boys say?

Mr. Brncich: So it's going to take several more months, even years, just to haul all the gravel! And most of the workers are volunteers? Young man, *(he directs his question to one of the shovelers)* Why are you doing this? Are you being paid?

Brother Matthew Leavitt: I'm not hired on sir. I just came to spend the day with my father and my brothers. Father has a team and Joseph and I are shoveling. We hope to be able to help at least one day a week until the temple is finished.

Mr. Brncich: But why then are you doing it? It's hard work, I can see that. Does your father insist that you do this?

Brother Leavitt: It is hard work. About as bad as hayin' I suppose. But no, Father does not insist that we help him. It is my choice. And I chose to do this because I know it is the right thing to do. I'm partial to doing what I know is right, sir. I was brought up that way. (*Men stop working and begin getting their lunch)*

Mr. Brncich: Well that's very commendable young man. A little unusual, I think, but noble. Are all your workers volunteers Mr. Wood?

E.J. Wood: Oh no. We have a few hired on and especially some of the skilled people who work at it every day. They have to draw a wage. But nobody does a thing like this for money, Mr. Brncich, we do it so we can have the great blessing of a temple in our community. We count it a privilege to do this work and to build this magnificent building.

Mr. Brncich: Well it's certainly the most ambitious thing I've ever seen.

E. J. Wood: Oh yes, it's ambitious, but our people never seem to chose the easy way. And maybe you would understand that young man's attitude a little better if you knew how his family, and the others, came to live in this country.   Do you know our history Mr. Brncich?

Mr. Brncich: I think I know some of it. But nothing that I've heard would explain this sort of dedication. I guess you'd better fill me in from the beginning. This project will be a monumental one for my Company and I'd like to understand the why of it just as much as the what and the how of it.

E.J. Wood: Very well then Mr. Brncich, let's sit down over here, in the shade,   and out of the way of these good workmen and I'll try to tell you how it came to be that these men tackled the task of hauling 14,000 cubic yards of gravel by horse and wagon from the creek bottom to the top of the highest hill in the area. *(They move to the edge of the stage and sit down, curtain closes on workers).*   You understand that our story is the story of a people driven from New York to Ohio to Missouri to Illinois to Utah by vicious mobs and uncaring governments. It's the story of a people burned out, thrown out, and robbed and hounded by intolerant neighbours, wicked politicians, unruly hooligans, armies, tyrants and opportunists. Until they thought they found peace in the Great Salt Lake Basin, the loneliest corner of America, a place no one else wanted. But even there the injustice and religious persecution followed them. But the story of Cardston really begins with the story of one man, Charles Ora Card. He was the most important man in the Cache valley, builder of the Logan temple, President of the Local Mormon Church diocese - what they called the Cache Stake. And yet, because of his religious principles and lifestyle,   he had more than one wife, he was a wanted man, hunted by federal marshals. It was a dangerous time, he was packing a pistol and never tying his horses so he could always make a quick get away. It reached it's peak of excitement for Brother Card on July 25, 1886............

SCENE 2 (THE ARREST)

(The curtain opens and the scene is the kitchen of a house, cut away so you can see the front and back yard and behind the house is a row of storefronts with various doors, The Logan House, The Tithing House, Telegraph Office, Law Office, Bank, and on the extreme end the Train Station. Card walks into the set and sits at the table, his wife Sarah Jane greets him and begins to fix a meal)

Card: Oh my dear Sarah Jane. How happy *(they embrace)* I am to be with you again. I was preaching up at Petersborough last night and I traveled with Zina, she went to her home this morning and I came here. I have been most watchful for marshals. Sterling tells me that there is talk of that lecherous apostate gambler Ben Garr being a marshal. And they say he is in Logan.

Sarah Jane: Oh, Charles. This is no life. Hundreds of men have been arrested in Utah this year for unlawful co-habitation.   And some who are convicted serve their sentences and then are immediately arrested upon their release and recharged. It seems so cruel and unfair to hold a man guilty for a condition.

Card: Well, unless something changes we will have to consider going to Mexico.   And make no mistake. If I am arrested I will escape if it is humanly possible.

Sarah Jane: But we didn't walk all that way across Nebraska, Iowa and Wyoming to get to Mexico!   It isn't right Charles, it isn't right. And now we live like animals holed up in our dens. And you wearing a pistol where ever you go.   *(She is very distraught)* And talking about escape, as if you were a common outlaw.

(We see two men approaching the front of the house

in a stealthy manner, peering in the windows)

Card: Oh come now, lets enjoy this morning together. Let's talk about something else, the children or (*Garr stumbles clumsily and noisily behind the house)* ...... Do you hear that?

Sarah Jane: Yes, someone is at the front.   Quick, Charles - Out the back, I'll see who it is.

(*Exum pounds on the front door and calls out for Card, Garr goes around the house and intercepts Card from behind as he gets clear of the house.*)

Card: Garr!

Garr: President Card, Sir. Stand and deliver. We are armed and hold warrants for your arrest.

(*Card seems to start running, but hesitates, obviously thinking better of it. The scene freezes and the lights come up on the Choir)*

The Still Small Voice

(*Pioneer girl solo)*
When your life is in the balance
Or you have to make a choice
There's a feeling that can help you
It's called the still small voice

It's a guiding light from heaven
Which affects men's happenings
But only if they chose to hear
And act upon it's warnings

(*Men sing having entered in front of stage)*
So as we see Card frozen here
We'll tell why the delay

He want to run and leave these men
But the Spirit whispers, Stay!

It's the still small voice.
It's the still small voice.
It's the still small voice.
It's the still small voice

(Women)
In just an instant he must decide
To follow his own fears
Or yield his heart and mind to
The Still small voice he hears

It's the still small voice.
It's the still small voice.
It's the still small voice.
It's the still small voice

(*Women & Children*)
To help you know these unseen times
We'll signal these strange actions
You'll hear a pleasant little Hum!
Each time they have impressions HUM

(All)
In any case what must be said
Is that the Still small voice
Will whisper warning, truth or love
But never take away your choice

It's the still small voice.
It's the still small voice.
It's the still small voice.
It's the still small voice

((Hum!)) (Card turns back to towards Garr, as he turns Garr pull out his pistol, Card reaches for his own pistol, ((Hum!)) but doesn't draw it. They stare at each other. Exum arrives through the front door,

whereupon Card puts his hands in the air as a show of good faith, then puts them down in a relaxed way and walks leisurely back into the kitchen, followed by the two men.)

Card: Gentlemen, Card is my name, Charles Ora Card. Mr. Garr, I have had the **pleasure** of your introduction, but you sir, *(turning to Exum)* you have my advantage.

Exum: I am U.S. Marsall E. W. Exum, currently assigned to the Ogden, Utah district. I am here with warrants for you arrest for unlawful co-habitation. I shall deliver you by the 3:00 p.m. train to Ogden for arraignment. *(He reaches clumsily into his breast pocket and removes a great bunch of legal looking paper and holds them up to Card)*

Card: Very well then, you will execute your warrant I am sure, but I was just enjoying a late breakfast with my wife Sarah Jane. Since we cannot leave the town for at least 5 hours. Perhaps you would read me my warrants while I eat my breakfast?

Exum: Uh, well, let's not bother with that while you eat. Go ahead finish your meal and we will read the warrants after that.

Card: Sarah Jane, give these gentlemen some tea and biscuits and they can join me.

Exum: That's very kind of you. Thank you Ma'am. *(Garr and Exum take seats at the table and begin to eat the food greedily)*
But before we get too comfortable, Mr. Garr could you disarm the prisoner.

Card: Well of course, I understand. I can help you out with this *(He rises from the table and carefully and deliberately draws his pistol with the men holding there's at the ready.) (Handing the pistol to Sarah Jane he says..)* Sarah Jane, my dear, put this away for me will you please. You don't object do you Marshal?

Exum: Of course not. The pistol is of no concern to me, as long as it's not being held by my prisoner.

Card: Well let's go into town then, if you please I have some business to do, if you don't mind. *(Card leaves abruptly with Garr and Exum gathering up their food and following clumsily after their prisoner)*

(The kitchen set is removed and the stage converted to a mainstreet scene by signs)

Narrator: (*Not a song actually, a chant, by two alternating men)*

(As this song proceeds the actions described are acted out on stage, and as Card visits different places the crowd around him grows. Evidently the whole community is aware of this situation and the number of people gathering around becomes obviously distressing for the Garr who quits the scene in the appropriate part of the narration, Exum becomes winded - he's portly- and almost has to be carried onto the railway car by the time it comes to that.)

As Card had a horse and buggy at ready
He drove from his house to the town
And Card thought he might make a run
In the moment his captors stepped down
((Hum!))

But the Spirit constrained him to wait
And he listened and quietly tied up his horse
Then he went to Telegraph Office and sent,
A message to, his lawyers, of course.

Next he stopped into the tithing office
With his captors along for the fun;
The Court house, the hotel, the Bank and cafe....
Then visited them all once more on the run.

Then one of his guards decided to leave
He had business of his own to attend
 (*Garr exits*)
But the time for the train had not yet arrived
So they took a long walk back to Card's house

Finally the hour of departure approached
By then all the townsfolk were quite in a state.
Their leader and friend was headed for jail
And they all thought to spare him this fate.

(*Crowd is milling around the train. Some passengers are on board. Card and Exum rush into the scene and go towards the ticket office, which is marked on the outside of the Train station store front.*)

Card: While you buy our tickets sir, should I not get on the train.

Exum: Well, You could..... No you'd better stay by me. (*Exum purchases the tickets and hands one to Card. They pass through the crowd with people shaking hands with Card left and right expressing sympathy. At one point Card is briefly separated from his captor who panics a bit and pulls his revolver,*)

Lorin Farr: President Card. We will hold him back and you can get away.

Card: *((Hum!))* Thank you brother, you are very brave, but that won't be necessary. Come Mr. Exum, let me help you to get aboard.

Back Stage: All Aboard!

(Card boards the train, closely followed by Exum. Card assists Sarah Jane and Fannie Paul to put their shawls in a rack, then he takes his own coat and folds it very deliberately and puts it on the rack, as he does so the train begins to move - director help us use our imagination on this - Card begins to visit with a man that he knows from Ogden (Elder Lorin Farr, my son-in-law's great great grandfather) the Marshall shouts from the front of the train that he has seats for them and for Card to come forward. Card shouts that he will be there "presently" but instead moves towards the back of the train, positioning two or three more people between himself and the Marshall ((Hum!)) and then he springs to the door, closes it behind him and jumps - the set freezes and he runs to the front of the stage, runs to the back, through the side and up the aisle and then down the aisle. He is absolutely breathless, stops and delivers the following lines, acting out his ride and his run and all the rest of it. Backstage cheers of encouragement where appropriate)

Card:
I lighted on the ground while the speed of the train was about 8 or 10 miles an hour, changed my course to the north and ran up the track across the street looking for a horse or buggy I could appropriate and discovered a young powerful horse on the east side of the street which as quick as thought I sprang into the saddle and turned the horse north and as the former rider was very long legged and not thinking of a duck legged fellow as myself using it on so short notice and without any ceremony, only grasping the reins from his hand, I lost the stirrups and the horse proved to be a young and powerful animal only partly broke and I found my hands quite full to keep him within bounds. It required both

hands to manage the colt and turn the corners which some times required the whole width of the street. I ran north one block ok amid the shouts and cheers of 3 or 4 hundred people, thence east 2 blocks, thence south 2 blocks thence east and south east 2 blocks down into Mr. Nelson's field used as a lumber yard. I tied the horse to the fence and ran about 25 rods and crossed the river into a dense thicket of willows. Distance

on horse about 7/8 of a mile, on horse and foot about one mile. The ride was the roughest of my life, the horse some times jumping 20 feet and me holding him my best with both hands. I feel myself a better saint than Lots wife for I never looked back. If I had I could have walked away as the conductor, I later learned, refused to stop the train, consequently it bore my escort away. I remained in the willows until 8 p.m. I sent and got my horse and buggy, a dark coat, and my pistol that I was ordered to yield in the morning.

Narrator: (*Lights go out on Card, up on Sarah Jane Card and Family - spoken except for the last two beats of each stanza which are done by the whole family as a vamp*)

The next morning Brother Card
Was so sore he couldn't roll over in bed
He bathed in alcohol for all of two days
To recover from his ride on the thoroughbred

But as he improved his physical strength
His spirits continued to fall
'Cause he knew that he must leave his Utah home
And it figured that Mexico would be his call.

But Card was a man whose report was to God
And before he started his southern flight
He visited the Prophet, John Taylor, himself
To confirm if his errand was right.

SCENE 3 (THE CALL)

(President Taylor, looking very old and tired is in bed, in a small room. Card is ushered in to see him by a secretary)

Henry Day: Rioght this way, President Card. President Taylor will see now.

President Taylor: President Card, what a joy to see you again. Living in the "underground" does not afford the social opportunities that we would like. I'm sorry to be brief with you, but I have other pressing matters to deal with. Please state your concerns.

Card: President Taylor, thank you for agreeing to see me without notice, and I will be brief. You may have heard that I was recently arrested and that I escaped. The pressure in Logan is unbearable. The marshals are everywhere. I borrowed a horse, without asking the permission of it's owner, or even knowing who the owner was, to expedite my escape and that man (Elder Aaron Farr) has been arrested for abetting my escape. I really must leave the area.

Taylor: I understand. Many are having the same problem. Where will you go?

Card: I have already packed my wagon President, and expect to begin the journey to Mexico within the week.

Taylor: I see. Mexico. Many have gone there. ((Hum!)) I wonder? No. President Card would you accept a call from your President?

Card: A call?

Taylor: Yes, I feel to extend a call to you to abandon

your desire to go south and to lead a mission to Canada to find a place for the settlement of our people under the protection of British Justice.

Card: A call?

Taylor: Choose two good brethren from your Stake to assist you and find the right place for settlement then return and report and we will call others to go with you back to Canada to establish a body of the Saints in that great country.

Card: A call... *((Hum!))* Thank you President. I accept the call. I know that you were born in England and lived for a time in Canada. My own grandsires left the British Flag to seek the freedom to practice their religion and now it will be my ironic circumstance to be returning to a colony of that monarchy to seek freedom from oppression at the hands of the very government that had offered freedom so many years before.

Lights go down on Card, lights up on the Choir

Narrator:

(sung by Zina and children and Sarah Jane and children)
Saints of Vision, led by the light
With a Spirit that cannot be broken
Hearts of courage on the road of faith
This is the trail of the Chosen

(Spoken by Zina)
Taking two new good companions
Card accepted the prophet's call
They went north to the Okanagan
Seeking land for the Mormons to settle.

They would call on the strength of the Lord

Ever seeking the Lord's inspiration
Praying for direction that they would find
A land chosen by revelation

curtain opens on ......

SCENE 4 (THE MISSION)

(Card is at a campfire with Hendricks and Zundel, they are in the wilderness of British Columbia near Osoyoos, October 3, 1886)

Hendricks: Well Bishop Zundel, do you think we should go home through Spokane?

Zundel: (*laughing*) And give those people another change to catch a bunch of "Mormon renegades?" I hardly think so Brother Hendricks. President Card, when we were trapped up in that hotel room, with no where to go and I overheard them plotting to arrest us in the morning, I thought it was just the right thing to do what you suggested.

Hendricks: That's right. We prayed that the Lord would make their eyes heavy and that they would over sleep in the morning and that we could escape before they even woke up. As hard as I prayed, I'll bet they're still asleep!

Card: Well, it was a great blessing how the Lord provided a way for us to get out of that circumstance. And he's been with us I know throughout this mission. And it has been easy and right to call upon his help when we have been so united and determined. However, all we have been able to determine so far is that there is no suitable land for settlement in British Columbia. I know the Lord has sent us here for a purpose, but it seems a curious result that we can't find the land we need here. We shall not go home until we find the right place, and when we do go home, it won't be through Spokane! Let's have our evening prayer now, shall we?

Father Direct Us by Revelation That We May Seek the Right Place

Men's trio _ Kneeling at the end of the day

Our Father in Heaven at the end of this day
We kneel together and humbly pray
For thy guiding light to direct our way
To accomplish our mission and never stray.
The humblest and weakest of servants are we
We know nothing of Canada, and where we should be
So we ask for direction to lead us to thee
And the place we can settle and ever be free

Chorus:
We cannot accomplish this task on our own
The place that we find must be shown
Father direct us by revelation
That we may seek the right place

Thy servants are hated in their native land
Arrested, imprisoned unable to stand
Because of our wish to live as a band
Of good Christian people, held safe in thy hand

We cannot accomplish this task on our own
The place that we find must be shown
Father direct us by revelation
That we may seek the right place

(John Taylor, across stage is seen singing this prayer)
Oh Father please hear this the prayer of thy son
Brother Card and companions are on their own
Protect them and bless them and show them the way
To find the right place for our people to stay.

(Taylor and three missionaries)
We cannot accomplish this task on our own
The place that we find must be shown
Father direct us by revelation
(Taylor only)

That they may seek the right place
(all)
That we (they) may seek the right place.

(After signing this song President Taylor exits, and the three are interrupted by Duncan McDonald a Montana mountaineer, best known for his exploration of Glacier Park.)

McDonald: Yo the campfire.

Card: Yo. Approach and be identified.

McDonald: Hullo. My name is Duncan McDonald. I'm from Helena, Montana and I've been walking all day, huntin' fer my lost mule. All my gear and grub is on his back so when I sees your fire, I thought I might ask fer some warmth and a drink ifen yer like to be friendly to a stranger in need.

Card: Welcome kind sir. ((Hum!)) I feel to say that the Lord has directed you to a place of comfort and refuge.

Hendricks: I think there's a little bacon and beans left in that pan.

Zundell: You can use one of my blankets for the night and we will help you find your animal in the morning.

McDonald: Mighty nice of you. What are you gentlemen doing traveling in this place all alone like this.

Card: Well, ((Hum!)) I feel to trust you with the nature of our errand, although it has been something of a danger for us to disclose it, at least it was before we entered this land of Columbia. We are seeking a land for settlement by exiles for their religion.

Zundell: You have heard of the Mormon's no doubt?

McDonald: Only that they all has dozens of wives, I think.

Hendricks: Well, the information that you have is highly exaggerated.

Card: But the truth is that some of us do have more than one wife and that we are now criminals in our own land because of it. We have been sent to find a place of refuge under British Justice for the settlement of some of our folk.

Zundell: But we haven't found anything suitable in Columbia.

McDonald: So you are Mormons. Well you don't look to have horns like they said you did, and I'm mighty grateful for your hospitality, but I'm sorry to tell you that you won't find what you are looking fer here in British Columbia. I knows these parts real well and there is only one place that suits what you are talkin' about.

Card: (*Hendricks, Card and Zundel move closer and give each other a knowing look*) Oh, and where would that place be?

McDonald: Why it's east of here, east of the Cochrane Ranch and between the American border and the Blood Indian Reservation. You would have to go across the Rockies to find it. I would take the train to Calgary if I were you and then go by horseback down to just north of the Montana border. The grass is as high as the belly of a horse in those parts. It's just perfect for settlin' I'd guess. Man alive, these beans taste good, I'm much obliged to you gentlemen, much obliged.....

Card: ((Hum!)) Oh no, Mr. McDonald, it is we that are obliged to you.

(Scene closes)

SCENE 5 (SISTER WIVES)

(In the large kitchen of the Leavitt home in Logan Utah. Hattie Leavitt and Ann Eliza Leavitt, wives of Thomas R. Leavitt are engaged in a quilting party with two or three of their young daughters, including Sarah Leavitt, age 12)

Hattie Leavitt: .... the area was just as McDonald had described it, and then Brother Card blessed the land for the gathering of Israel, both red and white. And then they went to a place called Lethbridge to see about the immigration requirements for our people. Then they ...

Sister Doolittle: *(bursting through the door and filling the room with her movement and noise)* Hello my sisters, hello. Oh you're doing a quilt and such a nice one too, not nearly as nice as the one we did last year at my house, but still and all, quite nice, and, well, nicer than I would have expected, if you know what I mean. Oh yes it's very nice. And Sister Hattie, how good you are looking too, and Sister Ann Eliza, well you don't look exactly in the pink, but then you never do, but you get along alright though, don't you? But enough small talk, let me tell you what I just heard, it is the most exciting news, it's just so exciting. You won't believe it when I tell you, but I just heard it and the first thing I thought was, well my good Sisters the Leavitt wives, they would want to know this, so, thinking only of you I came all the way across the city, just to share this news with you.

Hattie Leavitt: Oh, Sister Doolittle, you hadn't ought to have done that.

Sister Doolittle: Oh, you are so welcome. I know that you will appreciate my effort. I was thinking only of you and that you should know the very latest and...

Hattie Leavitt: No, Sister Doolittle, I meant what I said, you hadn't ought to have come over here just to spread gossip.

Sister Doolittle: Oh, but really it's not that much trouble. And what a kidder you are Sister Hattie, you know I never spread Gossip, it's just the latest news. And I know I said I made a special trip to see you, but actually I did stop at a few other houses. I am not afraid to share the wealth of information that I have you know. And I even learned a few more things of great interest. Oh, these are such exciting and interesting times, don't you know? Don't you know? Don't you just know it! Anyway here is what I have learned, and you must promise not to tell anyone.

Ann Eliza: Oh I think you can depend on that, we never breath a word of anything you say to anyone else.

Sister Doolittle: Oh thank you for your promise of confidence Sister Leavitt, and I know I can trust these children too. Anyway, I can hardly wait to tell you this, it's so exciting. But just listen. I have found out the names of every family that President Card called to go with him to Canada. And I'm working on a list of the ones that are going and then I'm making a list of the wives of the ones that are going and separating them into two columns. It's really just amazing.

Sister Hattie: I hate to ask, but two columns?

Sister Doolittle: Oh yes of course. One column for those wives that are going with their husband, and the other is for the ones who are staying home here in Cache Valley. Isn't that news! And tragic too. Oh the misery, Oh the suffering. Oh the humanity, oh the humanity! These families are suffering. They are being quite literally torn apart. I'm sure you never thought of that. But it's true, it's true. You better believe it. And of course, I should ask you Sister Leavitt, just to be neighborly and all, and it would never pass my lips, but I was just wondering, if you wouldn't mind, what is happening in this household? Is Brother Thomas going with President Card? I'm sure he was called, because I think someone mentioned that already, but they didn't know, or didn't want to say anyway, which of his wives he would be taking to settle in the land of exile. So then, my good sisters, which of you is going and which is staying? Or is it decided yet, because I really do have the third column you know and there are a few in it too, the ones who can't seem to make their minds? Is that your trouble, or have you made a decision?

Sister Hattie: I shall be going Sister Doolittle and my sister wife Ann Eliza will stay behind. It was decided last night. And, of course, we trust you will keep this decision to yourself. (*The Leavitt family members are sobered by the reminder of there pending separation and begin to hug one another*)

Sister Doolittle: Oh, I see. This is a delicate family matter. I'll be sure to keep it under my hat. Why only this morning I was talking with Sister Permelia Matkin and she charged me with the same thing. Not to breath a word about her family problems and I have not. Indeed I have not. Did you know that Samuel Matkin can't get either of his wives to go? He thinks he will go, but he has no wife to take. Only his 12 year old son Henry will go with him. That would make a funny pioneer couple wouldn't it? And let me tell you children something (*she turns her attention to the children and as she talks to the children the two Leavitt wives rise from their chairs at the quilt and move to opposite sides of the stage, away from the quilting and the gossip*) this isn't the first time in our history that people have been asked to leave the comforts of their fine homes and settle in miserable forsaken places. I remember when I lived in Nephi, when I was just a child like you, President Brigham Young came to a special conference and called a bunch of the men, right from the pulpit, to sell all they had and move down to Dixie to try to build that parched land into something useful. Well the girl beside me, she just burst out howling when her Pa's name was called. But I didn't even flinch when he named my Pa, cause I knew he wouldn't go, so it didn't bother me none. And that other girl, I tried to comfort her and to tell her that maybe her Pa wouldn't go and do you know what she said, and I've never understood it to this day! She said. "I'm crying because I know that my Pa will go, and I wouldn't have him for a Pa if he didn't go." Now isn't that a strange thing for a young girl to say. I've never understood it.

Sarah Leavitt: Pardon me Ma'am.

Sister Doolittle: Yes my child.

Sarah Leavitt: Well, excuse me for asking, but I so very curious....

Sister Doolittle: Well, some young people are that way aren't they, curious. They don't have a lick of patience or discretion. I was a little that way myself. When I was a child. Ask your question my dear.

Sarah Leavitt: Well, I was wondering. I seem to understand that you and your husband were called by President Card to settle in Canada with us, is that right?

Sister Doolittle: Well, uh, well, then, uh, well I guess you could, well, well, you could, I suppose it would be, well, I guess you could say that, in a manner of speaking.

Sarah Leavitt: Oh, Ma'am I mean no disrespect. And if you don't want to answer my questions, but I am wondering **so**. If you were called, then why aren't you going, Ma'am?

Sister Doolittle: Well, it's very easy really. You know that we have been mobbed and robbed and driven all across this continent and finally we have a little something for ourselves, and well, we think we have had enough and it's time for us to enjoy our lives a little. I don't see how God could want us to suffer any more. So we have just decided to stick it out here.

Sarah Leavitt: Oh. Papa thought about that too, I think, because he said that since we have come this far and obeyed the Lord so many times it would be a tragedy for us to give up now and refuse to obey. He said that wouldn't be enduring to the end. Did you think of that Ma'am?

Sister Doolittle: Why you.... A well, of course I thought of that. I thought of everything. I can't believe that God would want our family broken up and scattered hundreds of miles apart. That's what's going to happen isn't it. Have you and your Papa thought of that.

Sarah Leavitt: Oh yes, Papa prays about that all the time. He ask for the faith to do the right thing and then pleads with the Lord to someday knit our torn family back together again. I even heard him tell Ma that we might never be together again in this life, but that the temple could keep us together in eternity.

Sister Doolittle: Right. Sure... he's going 800 miles away from the temple and somehow that's going to bring his children closer to temple blessings. Let me explain something to you child. I know your Papa. He's a humble man, but he cares about his family more than anything and it breaks my heart to see him foolishly taking you off to the wilderness. If he would stay here and look after his family they might amount to something. People would someday recognize the name Leavitt all over the world, but if he carts half of you off to Canada and leaves the rest of you to starve back here in Utah, I'd be willing to bet that a hundred years from now the name Leavitt will be long forgotten.........*(lights go out on the quilting party and two spots on the two separated sisters)*

Duet

Sister Hattie: I'm a Sister Wife

Sister Ann Eliza: And it cuts like a knife

Sister Hattie: That I'm going

Sister Ann Eliza: That I'm staying

Sister Hattie: That she's staying

Sister Ann Eliza: That she's going

(*Together:*)
When we wed this man
We gave our whole selves to him
We have love, we have children
We have work, we have pain
But we have God

And we grew together
Like this quilt we have sewn
We are one, we are friends
We are family, we are sisters
But we have God

And our God has asked
That we tear these bonds
Hattie: I will go
Ann: I will stay
Hattie: You will stay
Ann: You will go
Together: We are Sister Wives
And it Cuts Like a Knife
That we're torn apart

Hattie: (*Speaking with music in the background*)
I was afraid when I married Thomas. Ann Eliza was so competent. So able. She was efficient, capable and was mother not only to her own children but to the children of dear Antoinette, Thomas' second wife who had died leaving Ann Eliza to care for 19 little ones, 10 of her own and 9 of Antoinette's! I felt like I was just another child and it was an uncomfortable feeling for a new wife to have. And I was a stranger too, and the ways of the household were unfamiliar to me. But Sister Ann Eliza accepted me and loved me, but most of all, treated me as an equal, although I surely was not. So now we are sisters..., sister wives, and our children are not strangers, they aren't even cousins, they're brothers and sisters. Ann Eliza and I have become one. And now our family is to be torn apart. We could all go to Mexico, or just try to hide out here, but the call has come and we have had to choose. Would we choose the right and listen to the voice of the spirit or would we deny it. We choose to listen. Even when it causes pain. And even when we don't understand it. I hate to leave and I feel that Sister Ann Eliza is mightily blessed to be able to stay here in our fine home, surrounded by her loved ones and our old and true friends. But I have the privilege to be with our husband. So the consequences are bittersweet for each of us. The only real peace comes from knowing that this is God's will.

Ann Eliza: *(Speaking with music in the background)* I was happy when Thomas took Sister Hattie as a wife. I was trying to be mother to so many children, and frankly, I needed support. And she has been a great support. Together we have been able to look after the family, dividing and sharing the responsibilities and developing a great respect and affection, not only for our dear husband, but for each other. She is young and strong and able to do many things that I can't do. I love her dearly. And it hurts me terribly that Thomas will be leaving me behind. But I know that Hattie can take the hard life, and it would kill me. I have not told Thomas that another child is stirring inside me now. I could not tell him and see the pain it would cause him to leave me behind in this condition. He might not even go. And he has never denied a call.

Sarah Leavitt: Oh Mama, I heard what you said. You are having another child? How can you possibly let Papa go while you are in this condition? I don't understand it. And you aren't even going to tell him! That's not right.

Ann Eliza:
At first I thought I could not let him go either. It seemed too hard. So I prayed about it and asked for strength. For understanding, for a blessing. And now child, ((Hum!)) now I understand. The Lord could have taken Thomas forever, instead he has only asked him to go a few hundred miles. He may even come back, or I may one day join him, but it is the Lord's will that he go now, and it is my privilege to support him as he goes. This is a very hard thing for all of us. Let's not make it any more difficult for your Pa than we have to. We won't say a word about this baby, will we?
(As Ann Eliza is explaining this to the child Hattie comes closer, the child fades into the background and

the two wives come together at centre stage)

We are sister wives,
And it cuts like a knife
That our love, and our joy
and our work and our pain
Will be torn apart

We are sister wives
We are sister wives
We're sister wives.

Lights slowly go back up on the quilting party

Sister Doolittle: ..... and then I asked him. I said, "what makes you think you can talk to me like that?" I was brave, I was. And I usually don't talk all that much, but I had something to say that day let me tell you. I didn't hold back anything. I wasn't my usual shy self. No not at all. And...

Sister Hattie: Perhaps you'd better leave now Sister Doolittle. It's time for us to put the quilt away and start our evening chores. Unless you would care to help us peel these potatoes and pluck a chicken?

Sister Doolittle: Oh, well, then, I guess I should be going. But I didn't even give you that list, and that's what I came for.

Sister Ann Eliza: That's quite alright Sister Doolittle. We know what we are doing, and that's all we need to know. Unless there is anyone on your list that needs our help?

Sister Doolittle: Well how in the world would I know that? I don't pry into anybody else's business you know. Why I would be like Sister Jones if I did that. Did you know what she did. She was...

Sister Hattie: Sister Doolittle

Sister Doolittle: ..... was asked to ...

Sister Hattie: SISTER DOOLITTLE!

Sister Doolittle: uh, yes.   Well I'm on my way .... to show my list to Sister Jones.

Sister Hattie: Good bye Sister Doolittle (*taking her by the arm and guiding her to the door*) Good bye Sister Doolittle and   (*she shuts the door and delivers this last line through the closed door*) thanks for ... uh... thanks for ... the ... news.

(End of the Scene)

SCENE 6   (SENA'S SONG)

The Scene is the temple cafeteria of the Logan, Utah temple   some time in   the late fall of 1886.   Sena Anderson, a worker in the   kitchen is   cleaning the tables and comes upon Samuel Matkin who is   sitting at a   table with dishes in front of him.   He is lost in thought and seems oblivious to Sena

SA: Excuse me... uh... pardon me.... Brother Matkin ... Are   you feeling   alright?

SM: Oh... what?

SA: I'm sorry to bother you, are you alright?

SM: Well, Oh... of course, I'm just fine.   I guess I'm   just a little   over tired.

SA: Oh yes, you do look tired.   The kitchen is closed now,   I was   clearing off all the tables to clean...

SM: Oh, well yes, of course, I'm so sorry. Pardon me.   I   am in your   way.   I will leave right now.   Please do excuse me, I was   just so deep   in thought, I didn't realize how late it was.   I'm so sorry.

SA: Oh, now stop being so apologetic.   You haven't done   anything wrong,   I'm sorry that I had to disturb you.   Maybe you could go to   another table, and I'll clear this one off so I can wash the dishes.

SM: Yes, that would be fine (he rises from his chair) but first let me   help you with these things, after all, I have been in your way.

SA: Thank you, but I can take care of it, and don't

worry. You really didn't do anything to be sorry about. But you did seem so very troubled, is there anything I can get you, or do for you? I could .. (he cuts her off)

SM: No nothing, thank you. ((Hum!)) But do you have a minute? I'd like to ask your advice about a small personal matter, if you don't mind. Well, maybe it's not such a small matter, I just need another point of view.

SA: Oh, of course. I'm actually the only one left in the kitchen and I have no appointments or anything, so I have all the time in the world. Tell me what's bothering you.

SM: Well it's actually very simple to explain. You know that President Card has called me to accompany him to Canada?

SA: Of course. I heard that he has asked over 40 families and that President Taylor has approved of each family and has urged them all to go with President Card to establish a Mormon settlement there.

SM: That's exactly right. And last week I spent hours pleading with my wife Melia to begin to make preparations to go with me. President Card has made it very clear that each of the men assigned to Canada is to take one wife with him. This is meant to be a permanent settlement with strong families. And my wife Sarah is too ill to go. So I was counting on Melia to be the one. But she will not go.

SA: Well that sounds too bad, but it's not your fault. That would be a good excuse not to go wouldn't it? You don't really want to leave this valley and your families do you? I would have thought that you would be happy not to have to go? I heard that only about 10 of those families that were called are actually going to go. You won't be the only one not to make it. President Card will understand if you wives can't go that you can't go.

SM: That's just it. I would be happy not to go, but I must go. I got the call from President Card last month and when he extended it the Spirit confirmed to me that I was to go. When the Spirit whispers I have made it my practice to obey. Now I've been in the temple for days, fasting and praying that Melia's heart will be softened and that she will agree to come. But that just isn't happening.

SA: So what can you do?

SM: Short of finding another wife, one who is willing and able to leave for the wilderness of a foreign country for a honeymoon. I can't think of anything less plausible, and yet I can't think of anything else. ((Hum!)) Who would marry me, with those prospects?

SA: I see...((Hum!)). Those prospects.... That sounds very difficult. Very diffic... It seems impossible. Um, .. *(She appears lost in thought _ lights go out on him and music comes up _ she moves upstage and sings)*

I'll Choose my Life Today

My life has been a simple one, until this very day
I was innocent and comfortable, at ease in every way
Although I've been a serious child and sought to do the right
No choice has been of consequence like the one I'll make tonight
When the Spirit whispers truth to me and gives my

heart direction
And especially when the task seems hard, with cruel implication
I still may choose to disobey, as many have before me
 But then I lose the promises that would have been so sure.
Oh   I can't deny the magnitude, it's plain in every way
And though it hurts it's clear to me
 I'll choose my life today.
Oh I'll choose my life today
 Will I listen and obey?
 Or will I turn away?   Oh No.
 The Spirit whispers this to me,
 I'll choose my life today

 Yes all my life there's never been a thing I've wanted more
 To be worthy of the promise of being chosen of the Lord
 I've wondered how he chose the ones to receive his greatest joy
 But now I see it isn't He, but me, who makes the choice
 Oh I can't deny the magnitude, it's plain in every way
 And remember that in simple things
 I'll choose my life today.
Oh I'll choose my life today
Will I listen and obey?
Or will I turn away?
The Spirit whispers this to me,
I'll choose my life today

(Lights come back on SM and he steps forward.)

S.A.: (*With hesitation but growing confident as she speaks)* Brother Matkin.   I have a confession.... I need to tell you something, it's not a confession really, it's more... more like a ....HUM! a testimony! The Spirit has whispered to me that I'm to be your new wife and go with you to settle in exile in the wilderness of Canada.

S.M.: I know!

He sings:
I testify the Spirit's voice has ....

(Together)
* We'll leave our homes and families and trust the Spirit's voice *
* And prove to Him we are His chosen, by making the right choice.*

  We'll choose our lives today
Oh we'll choose our lives today
 Will we listen and obey?
 Or will we turn away?
 The Spirit whispers this to me,
 I'll choose my life today

END OF ACT I

INTRODUCTION TO ACT II:

SISTER DOOLITTLE: Hullo again. They are busy back there gettin ready for the second Act. You folks should settle down too. Especially you people over there (*she points to where ever someone is still getting ready for the second act, even have a concession person putting things away and have her tell them by name to get cracking or something like that*) I just thought, well, since I don't have a big scene in the second act, and since everyone was kind of busy and all, well I would come out here again and see if you liked my big scene? Wasn't I great? That's acting ain't it? I was really emoting, if you know what I mean.

Anyway, the other thing I was thinkin' was that I could tell you a little more about this story. First of all. And this ain't gossip neither, it's news. Sena Anderson, she went and married that Samuel Matkin feller just a month afore they left fer Canada. And Henry Matkin, he was Samuel's boy, you remember? Well Henry he still went, but he went alone. Imagine a 12 year old child traveling without his parents. These were reckless folks. Reckless. Brother Doolittle and me we wouldn't never do a think like that. No sir. And most was like us too. Of the 40 families called only 8 couples responded and 4 other heads of households without any wives. The rest of us used our godgiven common sense and stayed put. Samuel and Sena Matkin, our happy newlyweds were so anxious to get out on the trail that they went ahead and left their livestock for Henry to take care of. Actually I think the pioneers were divided into 3 or 4 groups. They had to be careful not to draw too much attention to themselves, because the federal marshals were still out there.

I kept a record of all those who went and those who stayed and I was able to tell anyone that asked just what was going on, not that I was loose lipped of course. I was discrete, yes I was. The soul of discretion.

(*Off Stage.*) Where is Sister Doolittle, it's time to start the 2nd Act

SISTER DOOLITTLE: Oh, I think they must be ready. You kind of got me in trouble last time, I better not keep talking to you. I'd better go help them get started. Bye for now.

ACT II

ENTR'ACT

NARRATOR:
Saints of vision, led by the light
With a spirit that cannot be broken
Hearts of courage on the road of faith
This is the trail of the chosen

Of the 40 families called by Card
The chosen had dwindled to eight
Early in the spring of 87
Knowing that he could not be late

Card went ahead to Canada
To make the legal arrangements
He set two men to work with a plough
And surveyed his settler's allotments

Then he headed south on a saddle horse
And they greeted him with whoops and cheers
As he met with the northbound saints
Happy at last, together with fellow pioneers.

Filled with a great sense of purpose
Traveling in sunshine or rain
They were anxious to find their new homeland.
This was a glad wagon train!

SCENE 7 (WAGONTRAIN)

(On the trail in Montana. Card is speaking at a happy campfire gathering)

Card: Before I left we planted onions, lettuce, carrots, beets, radishes and potatoes, in the first garden in our new Eden. And brethren are there ploughing and planting oats and more potatoes.   On the way south I passed two groups of our comrades. Bishop Daines, Elder Mark Preece and   Brother and Sister Matkin are leading this parade of Mormon Pioneers to Canada and will surely be waiting some time for us to arrive.   Brothers Leavitt and Anderson are close behind them, but they are not faring so well, being burdened with more people and unfit oxen.   They are not making a good pace and I fear we may catch them before we reach our goal. *((Hum!))* We should remember their needs in our prayers.

I am pleased to report to young master Woolf, that I am the husband of the lovely woman he knows as Aunt Zina.   When I rushed to her wagon and took her in my arms as we met this morning for the first time in many weeks I heard him exclaim with great alarm.   "Ma that man is kissing Aunt Zina."   I commend you for your vigilance and protective spirit, my young friend, and hope that you will now accept me as one of this happy and faithful company. Now, before we have some music and dance I understand that Brother Farrell lost his horse again and had some adventures to recover it.   Please Brother Farrell tell us your story....   Where is Bro. Farrell?

Some Voices: He's over there.   (Right there)

Bro. Card: Yes, there you are Brother Farrell.   Don't be shy, come forward and tell us what happened.

Bro. Farrell: (from the edge of the stage where he as been sitting alone, reluctantly - at first - comes forward and tells his "story")

This cowboy's pride is in his horse
And this can't be forgotten
Cause if my horse has wandered off
I'm bound to feel right rotten

And this cowboy's boots weren't made fer walkin
I hate to hunt a horse that's lost
Than search my pony when he's wandered
I'd sooner off a bronc be tossed

But one thing's even worse than searchin
And that is being helped by others
You know the kind that likes to help yah
And then ever after that they acts like brothers

I makes me sore to be beholden
I'm sort of prideful, I guess that's me
I shudder to think of being grateful
To the one who finds my lost pony

So I keep one eye out for the horse
When my pony goes astray
And the other peeled for any do-gooder
Who chances to cross my way

Cause a cowboy with empty bridle
Can't pretend that he's goin' fishin
Strolling on the lone prairie
IT'S HIS HORSE THAT'S MISSIN

And if I sees a likely helper
Riding on the horizin
I will slip behind some rocks or bushes
Hopin' not to be seen by him

Well this was how I did my business
Up until a morning late last week
When I awoke to find no pony
She'd chose another day of hide & seek

So off I went with reins in hand
Hopin to find my horse real quick
When off in the distance I saw
Another horse, with a rider named Slick

Well the only faults that Slick possessed
Were his kind and generous spirit
He loved to do a favour well
And then ever after we'd hear it

So I were determined to hide from old Slick
It were my pride, I admit it
So spying a nearby chokecherry bush
Quick as a fox I dived in it.

Well the nub of the lesson I learned that way
Is one that I've ever since cried,
"When you dive for a low spot in bushes or trees
Be aware that the place could be occupied"

I lit on the top of a wild animal
It were scratchin' and squirmin' and tryin'
To tear me apart and it seemed at first
That it might be a Mountain Lion

But then I sensed it were too small for that
AND OH THAT SMELL
And I saw it were black with a stripe on its back
And it scooted off a bit and up went its tail!

The force of the blow of that gentle mist
Made my head and my stomach real sick
And knocked me clean out of the chokecherry bush
And lying there dying I looks up _ at Slick.

Now Slick sniffed at me from his seat in his saddle
Then smiled when he spied my empty bridle
And he said in his bright do-gooder way
"I see your pony's gone astray"

So Slick goes and finds my little lost pony
And leaves it for me, up wind, tied to a tree
I offered my hand to show him my thanks
But he backed up and wouldn't come near me

You don't soon forget the things that you learn
From a bout of skunk wrestlin'
And I'll share with you now
What was my great lesson

We all should be happy if someone is willin'
To help us to find a lost horse
And instead of hidin we should be a lookin
Fer the chance to get even, of course!

And especially while I'm still a stinkin'
Nothing would please more this cowboy who's sinned
Than to find old Slick's pony
And return it to him, from up wind.

Card: Thank you brother Farrell.   I understand now why you are sitting over there by yourself down wind in the campfire smoke!   Now let's have some music and dance before our evening camp prayer.

(A fiddle or harmonica player plays a little campfire jig as a few young couples dance and others enjoy watching and clapping etc. - tune of "Leave em Alone and they'll Winter Kill" then Pres. Card rises again)

Card: Brothers and Sisters, I   call upon Bro. Hammer to be voice in our evening camp prayer.

Hammer: Our Eternal Heavenly Father, We give thee thanks for our happy and united circumstances. We are grateful for a prophet who has called us to settle in a new land where we will be free from prosecution for our beliefs. We ask thy blessing to be upon this company throughout this night and to also bless our companions on this same trail. Especially we pray for Brother Leavitt and Brother Anderson and their families. ((Hum!)) Provide them, Dear Father, with the things and strength that they need to ....)

(Harmonica plays refrain from ...
Saints of vision, led by light
With a spirit that cannot be broken
Hearts of courage on the road of faith
This is the trail of the chosen)

SCENE 8 (TIRED OXEN)

(At another campfire in the early morning dawn.)

Thomas R. Leavitt: You awake yet Brother Anderson?

Johannes Anderson: Of course, Brother Leavitt. I've been awake for hours.

Thomas R. Leavitt: I can't believe I slept so well. I guess I was totally exhausted. We worked so hard yesterday to try to get those wagons up this hill. Even the little children were worn right out pulling on lines and pushing on wagons, but nothing would work. Those animals are just too lame and too tired to pull on this steep hill and in these wet and muddy conditions. I appreciated your prayer and your faith last night. ((Hum!)) I'm sure you are right when you say the Lord will Provide. I just would like to know how and when. If President Card and the main group catch up to us I don't think we will be able to keep up with them. We are too weak and too heavily loaded. We need this head start to get to Canada in time to get ready for winter.

J. A.: You are right Thomas. We have to get up this hill. The chart says it is 4 miles long and we aren't going to do it without a miracle. I'm sure the Lord Will Provide.

Samuel Anderson: Pa.

J.A.: Oh, you are awake Sam, what do you want?

S.A.: I heard you say that last night. "The Lord Will Provide." I don't understand how he can. Our animals can't pull these wagons. That's just how it is. Don't you think we should accept that? I don't see what the Lord can do about it.

J. A.: Well let me see if I can explain how the "Lord Will Provide" business works:

(*Anderson sings a song, (hey if we could get this sung with a Swedish accent I would love it))*
The Lord Will Provide

Whenever the day dawns in desperate times
There are men on the line of two opposite kinds
There's the ones who just worry, they're unsatisfied
And the ones who will say: "The Lord Will Provide"

When the Lord had commanded that   Lehi's sons
Return to Jerusalem and errands they run
There were some who were doubters and unqualified
And Nephi who said, "The Lord Will Provide"

When Goliath was taunting the Israelites
The army of Saul was full of fright
Who will fight the giant? Only one replied
'Twas David said simply "The Lord Will Provide"

When Moses reached the Red Sea shore
And Pharaoh's army approached for war
No one guessed the water could divide
But Moses said "The Lord Will Provide"

We'll never make it on our own
We've done all that we can do alone
The rest has now been prophesied
After all you can "The Lord Will Provide"

For this is what our faith's about
Hitch our wagons to God and let him pull us out
It's really just a simple choice
Will we listen to the Spirit voice
Or will we grumble and give up
And chose to quit when things get rough

Faith in the Lord will always win
Ahead of doubt and fear and sin
By choice then this idea I've applied
In times trouble "The Lord Will Provide"

Song Ends

Johannes Anderson: Now you boys go look after the livestock and I'll wake these people up and we'll see how
the Lord provides for us today.

(*the boy runs off stage, Johannes sits and thinks for minute, apparently saying a silent prayer, then begins to
roust the people sleeping nearby, Sam comes running back out
of breath*)

Sam Anderson: Pa, Pa, guess what?   Hey Pa you won't believe
this (*he realizes what he's said and says in a quiet voice*)... well maybe you might.

Johannes Anderson: What are you saying, is something wrong?

Sam Anderson: Pa, there are two big strong stray oxen in   among our cattle.   They ain't ours Pa, but they could pull   us up this hill easy. ((Hum!))

Other Anderson boy: Pa, Pa, The Lord Has Provided!

NARRATOR:
Saints of vision, led by   light
With a spirit that cannot be broken
Hearts of courage on the road of faith
This is the trail of the chosen

Oh the scene of joy and love

When the Saints the border crossed
Cheers of H'rah for Canada
Reached the heavens through the frost

With the wagon journey finished
Monumental tasked remained
To build a settlement from nothing
All these folks resources strained

The land was not completely empty
They had to deal with neighbours strange
Indians, traders and jealous ranchers.
Each would claim this prairie range

SCENE 8B (MA ARE WE THERE YET)

(Pioneer family crosses stage)

Boy: Ma, Ma, how many sleeps till we get to Canada?

Ma: It won't be very long now.

(Pioneer family crosses stage again)

Boy: Ma. Ma.   How many sleeps until we get home?

Ma: We're almost there.

(Pioneer family crosses stage again and joined by others who shout and give hurrahs)

All: Hurrah, Canada, We're Home, Hallelujah, We finally made it.

Boy: *(Moving to centre stage and addressing the audience)* If this is home?   Where are all the houses?

SCENE 9 (BUNKHOUSE/TENT Leave 'em Alone and They'll Winter Kill)

Dual Sets

Stage Right: Billie Cochrane's cowboy is in his bunkhouse with several other cowboys

Stage Left: A small tent on the banks of Lee's Creek is crowded with   Mormon Settlers holding their first Sunday Service

The lights are used to black out or highlight the stage area in use

Billie Cochrane's Cowboy: What a strange day I had, never seen nuthin'   like it!

Bunkhouse cowboy: What yuh talkin bout Slim? Tell us what happened to yuh.

Billie Cochrane's Cowboy: Well, I'll tell yuh about it.

(sings)   You know our boss is Billie Cochrane
And he's a fine and upright man
Son of Cochrane Ranche's owner
Always lookin' out fer the clan

Seems he heard that Mormon Settlers
Are squattin' on the Lee Creek lease
So he asked   Fred, Pete and   me
To run them off, restore the peace

So this morning we rode
25 miles to the Lee Creek land
On the way he gits real lathered
Telling   bout that Mormon band

He's talkin' how he'd send em packin'

  Back to Utah high and dry
And how he was gonna drive em
Home faster than a   blink of an eye

At last we stopped above their valley
Looked and seen em soon enuff
  We just stopped there on that high hill
And saw their wagons under a bluff

But as we sat and watched the Mormons
 Boss man seemed to change his mind *((Hum!))*
 He had been so mad and riled
 Now his face just got real kind

Lights up on Tent scene down on Bunkhouse.
President Card is speaking:

  Brothers and Sisters, thanks to the God of Israel that we have arrived in safety in this wonderful land. I know some of you were disappointed that it snowed last night, again. It being June and all. But don't that green grass look good poking through the snow! And I express my sympathy to little Sister Mary Lula Woolf who had her first and only store bought straw hat blow away in the western zephyrs this morning. People I have talked to from this country call that west wind a chinook and they say you must always hold on to your hat or tie it down real solid. I expect we will learn to lean into it too, in time.

I testify that we are in the right place. This is our new home. And soon there will be houses and all the other things that we need to make a stable and productive settlement.

We have made our peace with the native Indians. Their leader is the great chief Red Crow. He has given his word to me that we can live together in peace. I have made arrangements with the Government of Canada. I need to speak to the local ranchers and others to make sure that they understand that we are law abiding and that we will be good and honourable neighbours. I'll do that as soon as possible.

And because of this very wet weather we are now having we had to cross the St. Mary River in full flood. We acknowledge the goodness and mercy of God in lowering the water of that great river, just as he parted the river Jordan for the Children of Israel, so that we could pass through to our promised land, our new home. I want you men and women to record in your journals the great miracle that happened. When we got to the river Thursday morning there was no way to cross it. But after we fasted and prayed the Lord caused it to go down and we were all able to pass safely. Then we say that practically the moment we had made our successful ford of it, it went right back up to full flood. No one could cross it now. Praise God for his great goodness. He has lead us here.

Now I ask Brother Samuel Matkin to say a prayer on our behalf to give thanks for this safe arrival and to ask for the continued blessings of the Lord upon us in our humble and lonely circumstances.

Brother Matkin: Dear God in Heaven, The Father of us All, we give thee thanks and ask a blessing upon our little camp. Soften the hearts of our enemies.....*((Hum!))*

Back to Billie Cochrane's cowboy: Singing

Then he turned and said to me
Words I won't forget you see
Leave em alone and they'll winter kill
Leave em alone and they'll winter kill

Boss he wants to drive em out

But in a flash I hear him shout
Leave em alone and they'll winter kill
Leave em alone and they'll winter kill

Strangest thing I ever saw
The man's heart took a sudden thaw
Leave em alone and they'll winter kill
Leave em alone and they'll winter kill

As we sat and watched the Mormons
Boss man seemed to change his mind
He had been so mad and riled
Now his face just got real kind
Strangest thing I ever saw
The man's heart took a sudden thaw
Leave em alone and they'll winter kill
Leave em alone and they'll winter kill

Scene Changes back to the Tent:

Brother Jonathon Layne is Speaking: ... It has been a great sacrifice for each of us to divide our families and come these many miles. We have left the comforts of a well established settlement. ((Hum!)) But I testify that this country, this wilderness, will produce for us all that our Cache Valley homes and lands have produced for us. And that temples will yet be built in this country, I can see it as plain as if it already was here. I bear you my witness, in the spirit of prophesy that this is true, in the name of Jesus Christ, Amen

President Card: Now brothers and sisters, I believe what Brother Layne has said is true. All this will happen, but we must do our part. Now the first and most pressing problem is to prepare for this winter. We have planted some vegetables and some grain, and if God is willing we will have a great harvest, and we have brought a few food stuffs with us, but we can't possibly survive a Canadian winter without more provisions and without substantial shelter and fuel. This will require hard work and cash. I am familiar with our lack of cash resources. Can anyone suggest a way to procure money or work to earn some cash?

Brother Woolf: I move we pray about it. *((Hum!))* There must be work somewhere in the area, we can search for it, but the Lord knows who can provide and I say we ask him to direct us to it.

President Card and others: Right, of course, Let's do it

President Card: Sister Zina, would you lead us in a special prayer to implore the Lord that we might find work to do to meet our cash requirements.

Zina Card: Dear Heavenly Father, We thank thee for what we have and for all thou hast done for our good. We have serious needs and wants Father and we ask ....

Scene Changes back to the Bunkhouse: (Cochrane's cowboy is still singing):

As we sat and watched the Mormons
Boss man seemed to change his mind
He had been so mad and riled
Now his face just got real kind
Strangest thing I ever saw
The man's heart took a sudden thaw
Leave em alone and they'll winter kill
Leave em alone and they'll winter kill

(*Billie Cochrane enters the bunkhouse*)

Billie Cochrane: Oh, sorry to disturb you men. What's that song you were singing?

Men: oh uh nothing uh ...

Billie Cochrane: Oh it doesn't matter anyway, but Slim, I was just thinking. *((Hum!))* We're going to need some help to put up our hay crop this summer. With all this wet weather it's going to be a big crop and we won't have much time to get it off. You know where those Mormon's are camped, ride down there tomorrow and see if you can hire them to help us out. They looked like they could use a little cash, I'm sure they'll hire on.

Scene Changes to Tent:

Zina Card: And we thank thee again Dear God, for the loving mercy of thy son Jesus Christ. We know thou are our Father and we are thy humble sheep. Lead us to thy pastures, prepare a table before us in the presence of our enemies, fill our cups and anoint our heads with thy

living oil we humbly pray, in Jesus' Name, Amen.

End of Scene

NARRATOR: *Choir*:
Saints of vision, led by the light
With a spirit that cannot be broken
Hearts of courage on the road of faith
This is the trail of the chosen

Once established Cardston grew
Fruits of the work of the one's He chose
Out of nothing, bridges, roads, mills and ditches
Stores and homes and churches rose.

Thousands more would tread the trail
Shown the way by Card and friends
Seeking where to raise their children
Among the Saints where truth attends

And as the aged pioneers
Left this life from years of toil
There remained one promise given
Unfulfilled on Canadian soil

Listen now to two old settlers
As they meet to get their mail
This is the fall of 1912
Has their faith begun to fail?

SCENE 10 (POSTOFFICE)

(November of 1912) (Johannes Anderson and Josiah Hammer are picking up their mail and casually sorting through the letters as they talk)

Johannes Anderson: Brother Hammer, good day to you.

Josiah Hammer: And good day to you Father Anderson.

J. A.: Father Anderson! It's okay for others to call me that, but to you I should be Johannes. We are the only ones left you know.

J. H.: The only ones left?

J.A.: Yes, the only heads of households that came with President Card in the spring of 1887. The rest have all gone on to collect their heavenly reward. And we're slowing up a lot too, I see that you aren't standing for Mayor this year.

J.H.: That's right it's time to let that job go to younger man. Of course, I'm only 57 years old. I think you're a little older than that Father Anderson?

J.A.: A little. Try 83 years old.

J.H.: Well we have both seen a lot of progress in this little community haven't we? Remember how it was when we first got here. There was nothing. Now we have telephones, roads, bridges, irrigation, railways, mills, cheese factories, public buildings, a magnificent tabernacle...

J.A.: Oh yes, we have made a lot of progress. Thanks to Pres. Card and public minded people like yourselves. Three terms as mayor. You have been a great organizer.

J. H.: No, it was Card of course. And others. I haven't done much. But I do worry for the future of our little place. Card was such a strength, and now he is gone and so is John Woolf and all the others. How can we keep the people turned to God. Many of those people had met Joseph Smith, they were real pioneers. What will nourish the spirituality of the people without their influence? I have the same faith that I had when we came here. That God would answer our prayers and reward our faith. But sometimes I wonder how, and when?

J.A.: Yes, I know what you mean. I have prayed for something too. *((Hum!))* You remember how Brother Layne and Apostle John W. Taylor prophesied, right after we arrived, that this country would produce for us all that our Cache Valley homes and lands had produced for us, and that a temple, even temples, would be built in this country?

J.H.: Of course I remember that. Who could forget?

JA: Well the first part of the prophesy has been fulfilled. We certainly have all the bounties of the earth that we ever had in Utah or Idaho. This land has become our home. It's like it was our chosen land, our promised land. And practically no one even returned to Cache Valley, even after the Manifesto by President Woodruff and the whole the polygamy situation was settled. But the temple, when will the Lord Provide? I really have been praying sincerely that the prophesy might be fulfilled while these old bones are still rattling around. It's not just that I want to see it for myself, it would be so important for our children and grandchildren. This land really can't produce everything that the Cache Valley produces without it. Logan has a temple. The Lord's people must have a temple. I'm sure my prayer will be answered, but I just don't know when.

J.H.: Yes I know, we pray for it in nearly every public meeting as well. Oh look a letter from President Wood. He is down to conference in Salt Lake and he promised to write me if anything important was announced. Wait here a moment and we'll read it together.

(J.H. reads aloud)

Dear Brother Hammer,

You should be among the first to know the wonderful news announced by President Joseph F. Smith on October 4, 1912. To the surprise of us all, *((Hum!))* he announced that the Church would build a temple in Canada, and took a vote on it, which received the especial support of all present....

J.A: The Lord Will Provide!

End of Scene

NARRATOR:
Saints of vision, led by light
With a spirit that cannot be broken
Hearts of courage on the road of faith
This is the trail of the chosen

This will take us back to the first
Which we said would be the last
There we saw the children of pioneers
Working on a temple vast

SCENE 11 (FINALE)

(E.J. Wood is speaking to Mr. Brncich and the men are shoveling gravel)

E. J. Wood: So you see Mr. Brncich, these pioneers came to this area in response to a call. They chose to respond to the call and to magnify it. And those who did were rewarded by God for their faithfulness. This temple, to me, and to them, is a sign that the Lord has accepted their obedience and sacrifice. They are among his chosen people. Chosen because they chose to follow his promptings, his prophets and the good word of God as it was taught to them by their leaders. And we are confident, Mr. Brncich, that with the help of this temple and this legacy the children of these pioneers will continue to make correct choices for generations to come. At least we earnestly pray that they will. *(They move over towards the workers)* What do you say boys? Will you keep faith with your pioneer fathers and mothers? Will you follow the light that they followed? Will you have the courage to do the right, even when it's tough? Will you chose the right?

(Pioneers characters now dressed in white, and other players come onto stage and the lights come up on the Choir)

When the call is made to journey
To a distant promised land
Who'll embrace the challenge
And who.. will... make... the... stand
With the power of God Almighty
Saints of vision led by light
With a spirit that cannot be broken
Hearts of courage on the road of faith
This is the trail of the chosen

(Solo)
Throughout our lives there will be times
When as nat'ral men we're given
Choices like the one's we've seen
To obey the law of man or heaven.

(Solo)
When your life is in the balance
Or you have to make a choice
There's a feeling that can help you
And it's called the still small voice
It's a guiding light from heaven
That effects man's happenings
But only if they choose to hear
And act upon it's warnings

(Solo)
Were they working in their own strength
Were they carrying all the load
Did their faith begin to falter
With the trial along the road?

(All)
Bless us all to choose as they did
Bless us all to take the trail
Honour bound to heed the spirit
With God we cannot fail

(Solo)
If we're true to what they taught us,
If we follow in their ways
We'll take our place among them
We'll choose our life today.

Then it will be sung of us
As we proudly sing of them
Saints of vision, led by the light
With a spirit that cannot be broken
Hearts of courage on the road of faith
This is the trail of the chosen

This is the trail of the Chosen.
(*Take a bow, it's over)*

Made in the USA
San Bernardino, CA
01 October 2014